LONDON BOROUGH OF ENFIELD
LIBRARY SERVICES

This book to be RETURNED on or before the latest date stamped
unless a renewal has been obtained by personal call, post or
telephone, quoting the above number and the date due for return.

Pay Bed

Also by Nicolas Bentley

Nicolas Bentley

Pay Bed

ANDRE DEUTSCH

First published 1976 by
André Deutsch Limited
105 Great Russell Street London WC1

Printed in Great Britain by
Ebenezer Baylis & Son Limited
The Trinity Press, Worcester, and London

ISBN 0 233 96845 8

Contents

Illustrations

To
DOUGLAS MEARNS MILNE,
in deepest gratitude,
and because his was
the suggestion that
I should put it all
down.

The Wind in the Willows

It began with an absolute longing to belch and a total inability to do so. I could think of nothing to which I could attribute this. My wife, Madeleine, however, had her own views on the subject; she has views on most subjects. She attributed it to a combination of alcohol, lack of exercise and over-eating. To a suggestion so idiotic, a dignified silence seemed the only riposte, so I said nothing.

It was Madeleine's habit to refer to my uncomfortable condition as the wind in the Willows, that being the name of our house, and at first she was inclined to make light of the matter, but after a fortnight of watching my unsuccessful efforts at eructation, she could stand it no longer.

'Why don't you go and see Wooderson?' she suggested. Wooderson is our National Health apothecary.

'It's just a touch of indigestion,' I said. 'These things always come out all right in the end.'

'Well, whichever end it comes out of,' said my wife, whose conversation exhibits a decidedly coarse streak now and then, 'I should think it'll blow the roof if it goes on like this much longer. I *wish* you'd go and see him.'

'I tell you it's just indigestion. He'd laugh in my face.'

'That's always a possibility,' said Madeleine. 'Still, I'd go and see him just the same, if I were you.'

'I will *not* go and see him,' I said.

When I walked into Wooderson's waiting room the next morning it was crowded with the usual collection of asthmatics, geriatrics, epileptics, persons with boils in inconvenient places, little dears with streaming colds, others with persistent hiccups, a leg or two in plaster casts, on which well-wishers had scrawled their messages in lipstick and others had written vague obscenities, and the usual posse of chronic malingerers.

'Doctor will see you now,' said the attractive redhead behind the glass partition that screened the office from the waiting room.

'Me?' I said. I couldn't believe it. I had only been waiting forty-five minutes. It seemed unfair when others obviously in far more urgent need of healing than I had been waiting even longer.

'Yes, you're next.'

I went in; I stood; and I waited. Dr Wooderson, a man of deliberate habits, was sitting at his desk, filling in a form. Without looking up, he pointed towards a chair. The form-filling seemed to be a rather complicated business. He went on with it for some time; then, after reading through what he had written, he scrunched the whole thing up and threw it into the wastepaper basket.

'How are you?' he said, looking at me over the top of his glasses. He so seldom seemed to look through them that I sometimes wondered whether he knew he had got them on and was perhaps wondering where they were.

'Fighting fit,' I said.

'I see.' He got up. 'Well, good morning.' He went towards the door. 'How is your wife keeping?'

'She's well, thanks. In fact, it's she who insisted on my coming to see you. I told her there was really nothing the matter.'

'I see. What caused her to think there might be?'

'Well, I have a feeling of constantly wanting to bring up wind and not being able to do so.'

'Have you taken anything for it?'

'Just the usual,' I said. 'Whisky.'

'Right, well, we'd better have a look at you. Would you mind slipping your things off?' He waved his hand vaguely towards a high, hard and, as it turned out, exceedingly uncomfortable couch.

I took off my overcoat, jacket, pullover, tie, shoes, trousers, shirt and vest. I am a slow undresser and this took some time. Dr Wooderson waited, saying nothing, an expression of weary forbearance on his face.

'Will this do?' I asked. 'Or d'you want the full frontal nude?'

'That will do, thank you. Now, if you'd get on the couch, please – '

He thrust a stool towards me with the point of his toe. I got onto it and essayed an easy swing onto the couch. Unfortunately, I was slightly off balance. The stool shot away and I landed on the floor in a rather disorganized heap. Dr Wooderson lent a kindly hand to restore my bruised body to the perpendicular.

'No bones broken?' I thought I could detect a note of disappointment in his voice.

'I'm afraid not,' I said. 'Shall I have another shot?'

I got onto the couch all right this time and lay flat, trying not to squeal with laughter as Wooderson kneaded the more tender surfaces of my anatomy, whistling softly through his teeth the while, like a groom curry-combing a favourite steed.

'Does that hurt?' he asked, probing deep into the right side of my abdomen. I squirmed. I also giggled. I couldn't help it.

'Not hurt exactly.'

'Is it tender?'

'No, but it soon will be – AOUH!'

The moral of which is, never try to be funny with your medical man.

'Right, you can get dressed again.'

While I dressed, Wooderson continued his cross-examination. What had I been eating and drinking? How much exercise had I been taking? And so on. For one moment I had a brief, unworthy suspicion that Madeleine might have been getting at him. However, it was not so much the cause as the cure that I was interested in.

'No bones broken?'

Finally, as I sat before him once more, fully clad and in something approaching my right mind, he delivered his verdict.

'I'm going to suggest that you have an endoscopy.'

There seemed to be an ominous ring about the word. A variety of answers presented themselves to my mind. 'Over my dead body!' 'Exactly what I was going to suggest myself.' 'What the hell is a what-you-may-call-it?' Whatever it might be, I didn't care for the sound of it.

'Oh, yes?' I said. My voice sounded mysteriously different from its normal rich baritone. It seemed to come from rather far away, to have a sort of disembodied quality; an effect not altogether surprising after Wooderson's efforts.

'It'll mean your going into hospital for twenty-four hours.'

'Will it?' I said, 'And what will they do to me?' I loathe hospitals.

'They pass a tube down into your insides with a camera in it and take a few pictures.'

The off-hand way in which he referred to this passing of a tube, if meant to set my mind at rest, failed utterly in its objective.

'Couldn't I get my wife to do it?' I asked. 'She's got one of these new little Instamatics.'

'This is a miniature affair – it's no thicker than a pencil. It's done under anaesthetic. Well, it's not really an anaesthetic. What they do is to give you a hefty dose of valium.'

'Oh, do they? What effect does that have?' I asked.
'Relaxes the muscles.'

A superfluous precaution it sounded to me. By the time they were ready to send down their Kodak for a holiday snap of my intestines it was likely that my muscles would already be like jelly. 'That's why they like to keep you in for twenty-four hours. I'll get my secretary to fix it up, if you'll tell her when it would be convenient.'

I could think of no time when such a procedure would not present hideous difficulties.

'Right, thank you very much, Doctor.' Could those tones of feeble acquiescence be proceeding from my own lips? They could and were.

I went back into the waiting room, prepared to pour out my woes to the redhead, but I found I had forgotten the word that Wooderson had used. Estoncopy? That didn't sound right. Enstocopy? That didn't sound right either. Enscopity? Definitely wrong.

'Dr Wooderson wants you to make an appointment for me to have my photograph taken,' I said.

The redhead stared at me, her large grey-green eyes filled with astonishment.

'Come again?' she said.

'You know,' I said, 'they put a camera down inside and take pictures.'

'Inside what?'

'Me.'

The penny seemed to drop.

'Oh, you want me to arrange for an endoscopy?'

'That's what I said,' I said.

'Righteo. I'll let you know when I've fixed the appointment.'

'No hurry.'

'Couple of weeks, I expect.'

'Make it longer, if you like,' I said. I'm not one of those who enjoys looking for trouble.

As I drove home, I began to wonder how I should break the news to Madeleine. She's apt to take this kind of thing rather hard. She was in the kitchen getting the lunch when I got back.

'Well, what did he say?' she asked.

I don't know why, but I felt slightly let down that there wasn't the expected note of urgency in her voice.

'They're rushing me into hospital,' I said.

'They're not! When?'

'Probably in a couple of weeks.'

'I don't call that rushing you. What does he say is the matter?'

'He doesn't quite know. They're going to give me an endoscopy.'

'A what?'

'An endoscopy.'

'What on earth's an endoscopy?' Her ignorance is sometimes pitiful.

'An endoscopy? Surely you know what an endoscopy is?'

'I haven't the faintest.'

'Well, it's nothing really,' I said. I didn't want to frighten the poor girl. She easily gets the wind up and I could already detect those tell-tale signs of alarm that I knew so well: the anxious eyes, the furrowed brow, the convulsive clutching of her handkerchief; only on this occasion it wasn't her handkerchief, it was a packet of fish fingers. How was I to break it to her?

'Well, what they do is insert a little camera in a tube – '

'Oh yes, I know. I've seen it done on TV. Doesn't take more than a minute.'

She was back at the frying pan already.

'I don't think that can have been an endoscopy,' I said.

'Oh, yes, it was. I remember it now.'

It's no use arguing with Madeleine, so I held my peace.

Three days went by without any word from the surgery. I began to wonder whether the redhead was really as efficient as she seemed.

'Why don't you ring them up,' Madeleine suggested, 'if you're so anxious?'

'I'm not in the least anxious,' I said. She really can be very stupid at times.

'Well, I congratulate you. It's a life-like impersonation of somebody in a state of anxiety.'

'It's a bit unsettling, that's all, not knowing what's going on.'

It was another three days before the redhead got in touch. Everything had been arranged: I was to go into St Cyprian's on the 18th at nine o'clock in the morning and would stay overnight.

During the next two weeks the belching situation showed a sudden and unaccountable improvement. My eructations were now few and far between and I felt as fit as a fiddle. It hardly seemed worth all the bother of an internal examination if there was going to be nothing for them to see.

'I think it would be much better,' I said to Madeleine, 'if I were to call the whole thing off. It'll simply be a waste of time.'

'You'll do no such thing,' Madeleine said, in a tone of voice that meant there was going to be no argument.

The morning of the 18th was crisp with the first frost of autumn, as I got the car out, and the sun was doing its feeble best to smile through the clouds. I knew exactly how it felt.

'Well, goodbye, love.' I kissed Madeleine on the brow and turned to have a last look at the old house; then I got into the car.

''Bye, see you tomorrow.' Madeleine waved, then turned round and went indoors.

I swung the car out from the drive into the lane, then remembered that I had forgotten my pyjamas and toothbrush. A note of anticlimax crept into the proceedings as I swung the car back again, got out and returned to the house.

'That was quick,' said Madeleine. Her sense of humour is sometimes at fault.

'I've forgotten my pyjamas,' I said.

I kissed her again on the brow as I left and again turned my gaze towards the house as I stepped into the car. Then once more I drove away.

Had I known how long it was to be before I was to see her or our homestead again, my salutation might have been less chaste, my glance at our dear dwelling less perfunctory.

Entrance Exam

St Cyprian's is one of those hospitals that give the impression of having been built as a barracks or, more possibly, as a lunatic asylum, the influence of which, as I was subsequently to find out, it had not altogether discarded. It was built in bungaloid form; consequently the passages seemed to stretch literally for miles and were rather less than adequately heated, so that with the approach of winter they became admirably suited to the cultivation of the pneumonia virus. Anything that might have made the place remotely like a human habitation had been ruthlessly eliminated. Austerity was the keynote, except for the walls; they were painted in a dainty shade of *eau de nil*, calculated to induce instant vomiting in a patient feeling none too well.

Having parked my car in a space marked 'Reserved for Path. Lab. Staff', I walked with unfaltering steps to the reception area. Behind the counter was seated a middle-aged lady wearing what were obviously National Health teeth, though her glasses were as obviously of a different sort. They were made of a pale blue plastic material and the front of the frame was upswept at the outer corners, which were decorated with traces of diamanté. The teeth, when she spoke, rattled like a collecting box.

I was directed by this good lady to the Endoscopy Department, where, after a brisk walk of some fifteen minutes, or so it seemed, I again reported my presence. For a further twenty minutes I sat in an ante-room and waited. Presently a rather good-looking nurse appeared on the scene. She handed me a dressing gown.

'Will you go next door and get undressed,' she said.

Next door proved to be a cubicle in which there would scarcely have been room to swing a cat, had I had the forethought to bring one with me. I got undressed, put on the dressing gown, a hideous garment of multicoloured stripes that must no doubt have appealed to the taste of someone in the purchasing department of the Ministry of Health, but can have found little favour with anyone else, and resigned myself to another period of solitude.

This time, however, I had not long to wait. The good-looking nurse reappeared after a few minutes and led me into a bare and alarmingly clinical-looking room, a cross between an operating theatre and a bus station and combining the dis-comforts of both. In the middle of the room was a bleak, black couch. It was higher than Dr Wooder-son's and there was a pair of steps to help me to climb on to it. This I did, and then lay down.

As I began to recite the Lord's Prayer, a figure in a white coat loomed up from behind a screen.

'I am Dr Chatterjee. How do you do?' said the figure, in the precise accents that distinguish the conversation of those who dwell in the great sub-continent from our own sloppy form of speech. 'Tell me, have you had an endoscopy before?'

'No,' I said, and would have added, had I known what was to ensue, 'so I hope you know what you're about.'

'Well now, I am going to give you an injection of valium. You will just feel a slight prick, that is all, and then you will go off to sleep.'

Suddenly the nurse, who I had hoped would prove to be on my side, produced from some place of concealment a hypodermic syringe of a size that would have seemed adequate for injecting a two-ton hippopotamus, but which seemed decidedly too large to use on so frail a form as mine.

Dr Chatterjee, with a gleaming smile, jabbed the needle a good eight inches into my upper arm, and I knew no more.

Twilight Sleep

How long I remained in this blissful state I never really knew. What happened was apparently this (I piece the story together from various accounts, some more highly coloured than others, details being kindly supplied by Mr Dring, my surgeon, the house physician, the registrar, Dr Wooderson, the nurses in whose tender care I was placed, and my wife, who wasn't there): it seems my oesophagus, or more familiarly my gullet, was not as the oesophagi of other men. Somewhere it had a kink in it, which, when Dr Chatterjee started to withdraw his camera from my innards, fouled the apparatus and in doing so caused a haemorrhage, which, to be brief, precipitated the collapse of a lung, with other consequential effects that were decidedly uncomfortable. Of all this, however, I was happily in ignorance at the time and remained so for three or four days afterwards.

My return to full awareness was slow and partial. This, according to my wife, is often the case after I have been asleep, which no doubt assisted her to maintain throughout this period of stress that stoical indifference that was the admiration of her friends.

With the gradual return of consciousness, punctuated as it seems to have been by frequent lapses into coma, a series of confused impressions presented themselves to my disordered mind. I recollect a long period of what seemed to be twilight, in which misty figures appeared to be moving about, sometimes in a hail of confetti, at others in a pea-soup fog. These strange visions were occasionally illuminated by a magnificent display of fireworks and sometimes by images of the sort produced on a television set by lightning. So far as I could tell, those who flitted in and out of this scene did so without any set purpose beyond trying to disturb my repose; repose being at the time the one thing above all others that seemed desirable.

Among these flitters Madeleine featured fairly frequently. Once, I recollect, solace came to me, as I imagined, from the touch of her hand; but then I found I had been caressing a tepid hot-water bottle. I also had visions of old Mrs Yeo, who used to live in a cottage up the lane, going into and coming out of her back-yard privy. This was strange, as I had never actually seen her doing so, not being much interested in that sort of thing. I also had some difficulty in reconciling her appearance with reality, as I knew that she had been dead for at least a year. The redhead from the surgery also swam into my ken intermittently, though she later denied ever having been near my bedside (more's the pity); and

Dr Wooderson appeared, too, but he had been there. On one occasion, I became aware of the gleaming smile and neatly phrased apologetics of Dr Chatterjee. The face of Mr Clegg, the man who kept our local garage, also made one or two disembodied appearances; which enabled me the more readily to believe him when he also denied ever having been near the place. Once or twice I seemed to discern the features of my sister-in-law. It was as though she was bending forward over my pillow and was about to kiss me, at which point I mercifully lapsed into unconsciousness.

From time to time, various individuals in white coats seemed to materialize round my bed, usually in ones or twos. Some of these I seemed to recognize as doctors because of the stethoscopes sticking out of their pockets and the familiarity of their behaviour with the younger nurses. In another of these white-coated types I thought for a while that I could discern a likeness to the man behind the bacon counter in our local supermarket; and in yet another, the lavatory attendant at Paddington Station, a pal of sorts, the incontinence of advancing years making a visit to his establishment a priority whenever I arrive at Paddington from the West Country. Although at the time they both seemed real enough, I learnt from them subsequently that neither of them had ever been anywhere near St Cyprian's.

By degrees I began to sort out fact from fancy. For instance, what I had taken to be, in my semi-delirious state, a marmoset wearing glasses, which every now and then had poked its head round the door, beaming and gibbering, was eventually revealed as the matron. A moon-faced cleric, whom I had also taken to be a figment of my imagination, turned out unfortunately to be the real thing. It was his joyful task to slope about the place giving unction to those who felt in need of it, while at the same time producing covert smiles and gestures among those less reverentially inclined. His name was the Reverend Dobbs and he was a High Anglican. This much I deduced from his affectation of an ankle-length cape fastened with a pewter clasp, the crucifix that he wore on a chain round his neck, and the hot potato that seemed to fill his mouth when he spoke.

By a great stroke of good luck, after the failure of Dr Chatterjee's initiative, some anonymous benefactor had had the instinctive wisdom to trundle my inanimate form into a little private room separate from the Thoracic Ward; thus, involuntarily, I came to be the occupant of a Pay Bed, and was very glad of it. Meanwhile, the patients in the ward, those of them that were going to be lucky, coughed, oicked, gasped, wheezed and spat their way to health *en masse*.

Now, it is fair to say that so far as I was able to tell – when, occasionally, in an effort to restore my locomotive faculties, a pair of nurses would be detailed to drag me with trailing feet up and down the ward – it is fair to say that on these occasions it seemed to me that most of the other patients

Restoration of the locomotive faculties

would have felt themselves decidedly ill-used if they had been asked to change places with me. There would have been no more cosy chattering to each other, no more sassing of the nurses, and exchanging of football information with other patients, which seemed to provide all of them with the moral reinforcement that you need to survive a spell in hospital. Most of them, though far from juvenile, were reading comics; the younger ones were listening simultaneously to transistors. It was a heart-warming scene and one of which I wanted no part.

I know that to Labour politicians pay beds are anathema, that they are to be regarded as a divisive influence calculated to undermine the fabric of our society, and that the intention is to eliminate them altogether from the hospital system; and I daresay it would strike some Labour MPs as decidedly anti-social, as crudely selfish, and as a thoroughly bad example to others to say that you prefer a little privacy when you are ill, but that is all I ask for – a little privacy. Like Garbo, and just as intently, I want to be alone. I do not want to see or be seen by anyone, except, in moderation, my nearest and dearest. I do not want to have to listen to the groans, sighs, expectoration or vomiting of other patients; still less do I want to inflict these sounds on them. I do not want to listen or contribute to their conversation. In a strange, unhealthy way I would rather read or write, or *in extremis* even think; for all of which, in my case at least, some degree of privacy is needed.

And so to find, when I regained consciousness, that this was more or less what I had got was very heaven. I say more or less because the private patients' doors were usually left, not simply ajar, but wide open, so that night and day they might hear the reassuring sound of footsteps in the corridor outside, the comforting clash of trolleys, the bashing about of cleaners, the clash of plates and cutlery at mealtimes, the laughter and conversation of doctors and nurses, and the sobs of sorrowing relatives. All this, theoretically, cheered one up no end, and for a while I was regarded as the most surly of anchorites for asking that my door (these were in fact a pair of double doors, to facilitate the passage of trolleys, coffins, etc) might occasionally be kept shut. But, as in everything else, the nurses, dear, willing, angelic slaves, were always ready to oblige, and the privacy so much disliked by the Labour movement was mine to enjoy.

The Miracle Workers

In due course I began to attach their separate
identities to the various doctors who hovered about
my bed; to distinguish the Registrar from the House
Physician and the House Physician from his juniors
conspicuous by their zealous manner, unlike the
more case-hardened look of their superiors. On a
pedestal high above the rest, like St Simeon
Stylites, except for the absence of the matted hair,
the loin-cloth, and the demented aspect, dwelt Mr
Dring, boss of Thoracic Surgery. His satellites
assured me in tones of awe – and I was more than
willing to believe it, in the light of the miracle he
wrought on my ailing fabric – that he was the
greatest, the ultimate, the tops, with a skill in dis-
secting a rib-cage or slicing off a couple of cutlets
that might have been the envy and despair of the
carver at the Savoy Grill. Six-foot-three of handsome, virile flesh, with the muscles of a boxer and,
on occasion, the voice and manner of a sergeant-
major. He was a keen rugby enthusiast and his talk
was peppered with allusions to the sport. His two
principals assistants were spoken of as his 'scrum

half' and his 'right wing'. A successful operation he alluded to as having 'scored a try'; by analogy, I presume, an unsuccessful effort would have been referred to as 'one down'. Though he could – and did from time to time – put the fear of God into his atheistical staff, he was held in reverent affection by one and all. And it was easy to see why. No less than his skill in the techniques of the abattoir was his skill in diagnosis and exposition, while underneath the brisk, bland exterior was bubbling away a fountain of good humour. In contact with his patients his touch and manner were as gentle as a zephyr's and his voice as that of the turtle.

A string of minions was attendant upon Mr Dring. With most of them I soon became on friendly terms; friendly, that is, considering it was through their plunging hypodermics into my flesh, prescribing the most filthy-tasting potions imaginable, plugging me with tubes or inflicting other such indignities upon me, that we got to know each other.

First and foremost among these satellites was the Registrar, a Dublin citizen by the name of Dolan. His disposition was cheerful to the point of eccentricity, his friendliness to one and all a byword. His morning round of the wards was usually heralded by a distant sound of song, which, by the time it reached the corridor outside, would resolve itself into a full-throated rendering of the theme song from *Rose Marie* or a tzigeuner trifle from *The Gipsy Baron*. Sometimes he would reach his high note just as he attained the threshold of my room and there would pause to give dramatic emphasis to his dying cadence, at the same time wilting at the knees, then springing up like a jack-in-the-box. And it was not beyond him now and then to execute a few rapid dance steps, his repertoire embracing both the classical and shake-down variety. Occasionally I was entertained by snatches of recitation too, varying from 'The Shooting of Dan McGrew' to 'The Wreck of the Hesperus'. It was reassuring to find in due course that to these unlikely talents in a medical man were allied a first-class professional brain and considerable skill in surgery.

Dr Inglis, the House Physician, was a different cup of tea: neat in his appearance, in contrast to Dr Dolan's, which from time to time verged on the flamboyant; precise in his manner; and in his personality faintly lugubrious. I usually saw rather less of him than I did of Dr Dolan, but when he came into my room he brought with him an air of professional decorum such as I had been more accustomed to associate with the medical profession than Dr Dolan's ebullience.

Dr Robertshaw, the youngest of those who were in regular attendance at my bedside, combined in his manner an air of eagerness with an air of anxiety. His brown, bespectacled eyes seemed to show enthusiasm and perplexity in equal measure. He seldom walked, but proceeded always at a trot, as though hoping to outpace time's winged chariot. In contrast to the rather more philistine tastes of Dr

Dolan, his preferences were for Bach, Beethoven, Brahms, *et al*, and as mine were inclined in the same direction, there grew up between us a natural bond of sympathy. And I was glad of it. A few of the doctors, according to Susie, my favourite nurse, were real buggers; it was a relief that none of them had to do with my case. In the hands of Dolan, Inglis and Robertshaw – and not forgetting, of course, Mr Dring – I felt myself to be comparatively safe.

A friendly relationship between doctor and patient is the key, or rather, one of two keys, to a patient's progress and good recovery. The other key – and it is certainly no less important – is the relationship between the patient and the nursing staff. To make this a success there must be a willingness by both parties to co-operate with each other. But a willingness to co-operate need not be carried so far as to try to grab hold of every pretty nurse who happens to pass your sick-bed, as I gather was the habit of some patients in the ward, as soon as they felt like taking a bit of exercise. Nor need you seek to caress a nurse who is taking your temperature or removing a bed-pan. There are too many ways in which a nurse who is subjected to this kind of thing can get her own back. A bed-pan is not the most comfortable of receptacles for a patient to have to use, and to be stuck with it for half an hour after you have finished with it can be decidedly awkward. Again, you do not expect hospital food to be up to

Cordon Bleu standards, but even such unappetizing stuff is less revolting if it is served hot and promptly than if it comes to you tepid and after a long wait; and a patient who is used to being injected, especially in the more tender regions of the thigh or bottom, will be well aware of the difference between the use of a sharp needle and a blunt one. By employing these and other minor forms of torture, any nurse at St Cyprian's would have had it in her power to retaliate against a patient who was an habitual trouble-maker. Yet I never heard of a nurse taking advantage of her situation, not even from among those few with a reputation for being somewhat stern or having their particular likes and dislikes among the patients.

Nurses seem to come in four shapes and sizes: the Student Nurse, the lowliest form of nursing life, though none the less willing and efficient for all that; the Nurse *per se*, who, because of the direct nature of her contact with the patient, can make or mar his stay in hospital; and a higher form of life known as the Staff Nurse. There is also something called the Auxiliary Nurse. Auxiliaries are often ladies who have retired, but are not averse to a little part-time work and usually get pushed into such unrewarding occupations as doing night duty or performing other tedious chores. Then, on a level more exalted than all the rest, stand the Sisters, one to each ward; their responsibilities are heavy, their word is law, and don't you forget it. Each of these categories is distinguished from the others by minor variations in their gear and by the duties allotted to them.

The staff nurses, three in number, were a cheerful crew. Sally, the youngest, had the most sex appeal; not that she set out to exploit it. She didn't have to: nature had endowed her with a face and form that would have produced fatal effects had she been in the Cardiac instead of the Thoracic Ward.

Jean was a little older, a little more sedate, a little more experienced, but still a bundle of fun when time and opportunity allowed for a bit of back-chat.

And finally there was O'Grady. If she had a Christian name, I never heard anyone use it. She was rather older than the other two and had been a staff nurse, so she said, for more years than she could remember. Her outlook on life was incurably optimistic. Even death seemed scarcely to modify her cheerfulness and her jokes were full of coffin humour. She had a simple philosophy of life, but one not to be disputed: 'If you're alive, you're alive; if you're dead, you're dead, and there's damn all you can do about it either way.' Her appearance in the ward was usually signalled by a call, in the richest of brogues, that could be heard at the far end of the corridor: 'Watch it, boys, O'Grady's back on the beat!' or sometimes, 'O'Grady's on the way, boys, budge up in bed!' If her manner was a little out of the ordinary, she was certainly the kindest and the best of nurses.

How lucky I was that, with few exceptions, those in whose hands destiny had placed my shattered form were angels of mercy: gentle, willing, patient and unfailingly agreeable. I think of them now as sanctified, with little golden haloes poised above their starched caps. In my mind's eye, I see them still performing with tenderness and discretion the more disgusting chores which the nursing of a helpless invalid involves. Once again I listen to their *sotto voce* expletives as they struggle with some awkward bit of apparatus attached to my person in order to aid my recovery. I see their shining morning faces – no, that is an exaggeration: I see them in the early morning trudging in after a hard night at the disco, sleepy-eyed and weary of limb, yet quite unaccountably cheerful and ready for an equally hard day's work in the ward. Mary, Maureen, Sandra, Deirdre, Sarah, Dawn (Hopeless Dawn, as they used to call her), Yvonne, Susie – especially Susie, I salute you one and all, my pretty dears.

Human nature being what it is, and feminine human nature in particular, it is unwise for a patient, if of the male sex, to allow himself to feel, or at any rate disclose, a partiality for any particular nurse. But Susie's case was different. From the first, while I was still barely conscious, if at all, I was allocated to her care, and my recovery became to her as the Holy Grail to Siegfried; or perhaps more appropriately, as Women's Lib to Miss Germaine Greer. I do not doubt she would have felt the same proprietory right in any other patient who might happen to have been wheeled in. It was simply that she was born to her calling, and, I suspect, could not but

O'Grady

39

show a deep devotion to any patient that came her way; and I was both glad and fortunate to have someone always at hand so willing, so kind and so cheerful.

The Jam Jar

One of the first things I became aware of after attaining a state of semi-consciousness, or, as my wife would have put it, returning to normal, was that certain liberties had been taken with my person. To my dismay, I discovered that mid-way between the ribs on the right side of my body a length of rubber tubing had been inserted, the other end of which drained into a large glass jar, sealed at the top and half full of some disgusting liquid matter. In colour and consistency it looked like gruel, but not even Oliver Twist would have asked for more. This putrid stuff, it seemed, was collecting in my lung and being syphoned off into the jar by a little pump. A rather ingenious arrangement, I thought.

This jar, commonly referred to by the nurses as my 'jam jar', was an object of the deepest fascination to Mr Dring and his team. For the ward sister, too, it seemed to have a peculiar interest. Mr Dring, either by himself or with the sister or one of the doctors, would sometimes sit for long minutes together silently contemplating the jar, and occasionally giving it a kick or a shake. Sometimes they seemed well satisfied with my rate of discharge; at others gloom settled upon their faces. On one such occasion, as their expressions became more and more grave, I suggested that pen and paper should be sent for, that I might prepare my last will and testament. This jest, however, was not well received.

Continuing to pursue cautiously the examination of my weakened form to see what other outrages had been perpetrated upon it, I found that some person or persons unknown had inserted another tube into, of all places, the back of my right hand, which had been punctured for the purpose by some blunt instrument and was now strapped to a splint. I never rightly understood what this tube was for, and fearing that if I did know it might seriously retard my recovery, I never asked.

At this point I began to wonder whether I might not have fallen into the clutches of some mad physician, a sort of second cousin to Dr Who. This suspicion was temporarily confirmed when I found that, not content with having pushed the garden hose into my right side, someone had pushed another tube into the biceps of my left arm. This also went into a bottle, one that was suspended overhead. I was told that this was a saline drip; a phrase of which I made a mental note as fitly describing a gormless nephew of mine serving in the Royal Navy.

For some reason or other, my main tube – the one in my side, of which I was proudest when showing off this elaborate plumbing system to interested visitors – never seemed to work properly for very long. This, however, had its compensations, if not for me, for Dr Dolan, because it enabled him to keep his hand in by constantly pulling the tube out and inserting it somewhere else. In this he took a keen delight, repeating the process some four or five times and ending up by giving me a rather chic little contraption attached to the upper part of my right shoulder-blade. On these occasions a local anaesthetic was said to be used, but being, as a rule, in no position to see what was going on, I had to accept Dr Dolan's word for it. At any rate, it didn't seem to work very well and to Dr Dolan's rendering of Pinkerton's famous aria from *Madame Butterfly* I frequently added a caterwauling obbligato of my own.

On the occasion, I think, of the third of these experiments, an amusing incident occurred. Dr Dolan, suspecting that he was nearing the seat of the trouble, had removed the tube preparatory to sticking it in somewhere else. Before plugging the hole, and with the object of ensuring that he was on the right tack, he asked me to give a cough, 'a good, loud cough'. I did so, and from the open wound shot a veritable cascade of matter so evil smelling that not only Dr Dolan, but Susie and Sandra, who were assisting him, were virtually overcome, as well as drenched. How I laughed!

But not for long. The tube was reinserted higher up and the pumping process began all over again.

Frankly, I found all this business of tubes and jars and pumps rather undignified. I felt that it reduced my case, which I took to be one of rather special interest, to the level of a problem in hydraulics. But the greatest indignity of all came from yet another tube which, without so much as a 'by your leave', someone had shoved up my nose; to be precise, into my left nostril. I am well aware that by classical standards my nose could hardly be described as a thing of beauty, much less a joy for ever, especially during the hay fever season; but that it should have been thought that anyone might use it as a repository for any old bit of rubber tubing they happened to have left over did at first seem a bit hard. However, there was method in their madness: the delicate state of my oesophagus made it inexpedient to feed me by mouth; my nose, therefore, really seemed the only alternative. This, of course, placed certain restrictions on my diet. Oysters, plovers' eggs, smoked salmon and caviar were out. I rather regretted this, as I had hardly tasted any of them since the purchasing power of the £ had been placed on the slip-way and given a push.

Now, why it should be I don't know, but food, or rather, drink, when absorbed through the nasal passage seems to me to lose something of its savour. It becomes, in a word, nauseating. But if, in time, no alternative presents itself, familiarity will usually breed content, even with the most unpleasant circumstances. I don't say that I ever got to the stage of preferring a nasal intake of luke-warm carrot soup to a nice hot plate of the real thing, but I did reach a stage at which I came to accept such fare without the harsh words and still harsher gestures that at first marred my relationship with the nurses who tried to feed me. Eventually, Horlicks, Complan, Ribena, tea, coffee, cocoa and soups of a dozen different varieties were coursing through my nose with the ease of mucous during a heavy cold.

None of these beverages, nourishing and succulent though they were supposed to be, seemed to have much taste, but that was beside the point. If ever the Body Beautiful was to be restored to its former elegance – and it did not take long for it to be reduced to the semblance of an Indian fakir's – it was essential, according to the dietary pundits, that the demoralizing process of the drip-feed should be gone through every four hours.

It wouldn't have been so bad, perhaps, if the various tubes and valves that formed part of my feeding apparatus had worked properly, but they were continually getting clogged or breaking down, and it was the exception rather than the rule for me to have an uninterrupted meal. It might start off all right, but then would come a sudden cessation of sustenence: oxtail soup would cease to trickle through the pharynx and nurses would gather round, trying to put the thing right. Sometimes the stoppage would last for only a few minutes, at others for half an hour or so; then, just as I had got used to the prospect of gradual starvation, with a sudden splurge the supply of oxtail would be resumed. At other times, the apparatus packed up altogether, leaving me faint and famished from lack of nasalized cocoa. On such occasions, oaths and execrations reverberated round my bedhead as the nurses tried to repair the damage. I have a great deal to thank them for, my dear, devoted nurses, not least for the extension of my vocabulary. Words of which I scarcely knew the meaning, and some indeed that were altogether new to me, went ringing round the room.

The same sort of trouble as that which seemed to afflict my feeding arrangements occurred with the drainage tube through which the stuff that accumulated in my lung was discharged into the jar beside my bed. In order to deal with this outflow of sewage, my room was converted into a miniature pumping station. In the stopper of the jar were two tubes: one of these was the one that was connected to my trunk; the other was connected to the pump already mentioned, which in turn was connected to a plug in the wall. From this ingenious circuit, however, the pump seemed to get little joy. It was continually in a state of revolt and having to be exchanged for another pump, which, with luck, might be expected to stay in operation for twenty-four hours, but would more probably pack up after twenty-five minutes. Thus was I provided with a constant diversion, so necessary to the well-being of morale in hospital. Just as I had settled down for a post-prandial nap, after a delicious nasal douche of cold consommé, there would be an ominous clunk and the pump would grind to a halt.

I was constantly being assured that it was essential for the pump to be kept going, otherwise the accumulation of muck in my lung would swiftly overwhelm my already enfeebled powers of resistance, with the possibility of dire consequences. So whenever I heard the pump cut out, I would search frantically for the bell that was supposed to be pinned to my sheets and within easy reach. Often it was pinned so far down the bed or so high up on my pillow that I could have got at it only at the cost of bursting my stitches or dislodging one of the tubes that had by now settled down so comfortably into their allotted places in my anatomy. All I could do was to try and shout for help. But here there was a difficulty. The damage to my oesophagus and the resulting weakness and debility had so reduced the powers of speech that all I could do was to produce a sound like the cawing of a rook. Now, it so happened that close to the wing where I was incarcerated was a clump of trees, which I could see from my window, where an enormous colony of rooks had established themselves. Several of the creatures were usually to be seen stalking about with an air of idiotic majesty on a small grass plot that separated the ward I was in from the one next door. Their incessant croaking and cawing had so anaesthetized the ears of the nursing staff that my own pathetic efforts to raise a cry often went unheeded for half an hour or longer.

When at last my plea was heard, a nurse, or possibly the Ward Sister herself, would come charging in.

'YES – what is it?'

'I'm afraid my pump's packed up again.'

'Oh, is *that* all?'

She would then begin to wrestle with the pump, and if unable to bring it to life, would send for another.

Deirdre of the Sorrows

Lying in bed, either alone or in company with someone else, is normally one of man's most enjoyable occupations. That joy, however, is considerably abated if you have a hefty length of rubber tubing inserted into your side, another length in your left bicep, your right arm in a splint, and your nose plugged with a nasal drip. Add to this a stern injunction by the powers that be never to cross your ankles, much less your legs – against the peril of inducing thrombosis – and the pleasures of the couch virtually cease to exist.

In such a case, the added inconvenience of a pump may not seem to be of much significance, but it was one of which I could not fail to be aware. No less of an anxiety was my 'jam jar'. As I have explained, in the stopper of this jar there were two tubes; one was the tube connecting it with the pump, the other the tube connecting it with me. I soon learnt, since my very existence seemed to depend on it, that it was vital that the tube connected with the pump should *on no account* be removed (as was necessary when either the jar or the pump had to be changed) without first ensuring that the other tube had been clamped off. Failure to observe this precaution, I was told, would result in air rushing into the patient, who would then blow up.

I did not care for the rather nonchalant way in which some of the nurses handled the jar when it needed to be removed and another put in its place. Some would pluck out the tube with an abandon that seemed to reek of disaster, chatting and laughing as they did so. One young nurse, a clumsy, buxom creature, had an insouciant approach to the procedure which would have put the fear of God into me, if I had not considered Him to be, after David Frost, non-person No. 1. The name of this carefree young thing was Deirdre. She was a jolly girl with a face that was permanently wreathed in smiles. Deirdre of the Sorrows, I called her.

'Do you know about Yeats?' I asked her one day, in an unguarded moment.

'Oo, aren't they *marvellous*!' she said, 'I've just got their new record.'

'I think we must be talking at cross-purposes,' I said.

'It's the group I mean – come on, you *must* know them.'

'Group of what?' – as if I didn't know; still, I was determined to go down fighting.

'*Singers*. Four fellers and a girl. They're *great*.'

'Well, the Yeats I was talking about wasn't too bad.'

'What does he do, then?'

'He was a writer; a famous poet.'

She looked at me for a moment, lost in thought, so far as she was capable of it.

'I suppose you must be terribly clever really, aren't you?' she said reflectively.

I cast my eyes upon the blanket. 'I suppose I must be,' I said.

'I mean, knowing all that about books and things.'

'Oh, anyone can learn about books,' I said. 'It's the things that are difficult.'

'How j'you mean?'

'The getting through life. That, Deirdre my love, is the acid test.'

She looked puzzled. 'I don't get it. What are you on about?'

'Well,' I said:

'Whether 'tis nobler in the mind to suffer
 The slings and arrows of outrageous fortune,
 Or to take arms against a sea of troubles,
 And by opposing, end them.'

She looked at me with a mystified expression. 'You know, some days,' she said, 'I think you're stark bonkers, I do, honestly.'

It was not long after we had had this stimulating exchange that there was more trouble with the pump. Deirdre came into my room to swap it for another and she knelt beside the bed, tugging away at the tube to disconnect it from the jar. The two tubes were always inserted into the stopper firmly, so as to avoid either of them being pulled out by accident. She had almost succeeded in getting the tube out when I realized that not only had she failed to clamp me off the tube that extruded from my side, but that this was the one she was pulling out, instead of the tube connected with the pump.

'For God's sake! Have a care, woman!' screamed I.

'Eh?' said Deirdre.

'You're pulling out the wrong one.'

She stared in a bemused fashion at the tube she was grasping in her hand, then followed it with her eyes to where it disappeared underneath the bedclothes.

'Gawd, you're right,' she said, beaming from ear to ear.

'*And* you forgot to clamp me off.'

'Christ, I never! – ' Then, as she verified the fact, 'Would you *believe* it?' she said, and collapsed in a turmoil of laughter.

'It isn't as funny as all that,' I said. 'Perhaps you'd better ask Sister to have a go at it.' Though my dignity was somewhat impaired by my nasal drip, I think she got the message. At any rate, she slowly picked herself up off the floor and, still convulsed with laughter, tottered from the room.

Deirdre was the only nurse I came across who showed quite such an air of abandon towards her sacred calling. There were times when her jollity was welcome, indeed, infectious; but I did find eventually that her incessant mirth had a tendency to pall, particularly on such occasions as when I found it necessary to ask her for a bed-pan. This she seemed to find no end of a joke and would advance into the room tootling as though she were playing a trumpet and beating the pan like a drum.

In course of time my condition so far improved that recourse to the bed-pan was abandoned in favour of my making my way to the lavatory. But this was only after several weeks of the indignity of the bed-pan routine. I could never work up quite the same attitude of jocularity towards this as nurses and sisters showed towards it. Had I been on the receiving end, as you might say, instead of at the opposite pole, I might have shared their point of view. As it was I sat there listening to their banter.

'I never knew anyone take so *long*.'

'Like a newspaper while you're waiting?'

'You gone to sleep on that thing?'

Such comments, made with excellent intent and the cheerfulness that is supposed to cement the relationship between nursing staff and patients, did not, in practice, ease my situation. That I could only do for myself.

Going to the lavatory involved my passing

through the ward; a journey that would have been easier and less calculated to arouse facetious comment had I been free of the encumbrance of my jar. But so long as I had a tube in my side, the jar had to go wherever I went.

As I staggered from my room with uncertain steps, toting this incubus at my side on the end of a cord, and made my way by fits and starts along the ward, the cries and greetings of the patients, though apt and sometimes encouraging, I could have done without. Yet they served in the end to establish a kind of *rapport* between us. I could not escape the feeling at first that because of my self-selected isolation they were inclined to regard me as toffee-nosed; a suspicion, as it turned out, that was quite unworthy. This was proved by the willing hands that came to my assistance whenever I fell over, which I did frequently, or slid to the ground under the weight of my miserable jar.

My appearance at the door of my room was usually a signal for the wits of the ward to get to work and the place would soon be echoing with their merry quips.

"ere comes the 'okey-pokey man!' (It's true, the jar looked not unlike the sort of container from which ice cream might have been dispensed.)

'Give us a taste, mate.'

"ow's yer goldfish gettin' on then?'

'You know what you ought to do with that, don't you? Put it on matron's asparagus.'

'*Give us a taste, mate*'

I would willingly have emptied the jar over their heads, but that it was clear their witticisms were well-intentioned.

Sister Forbes

I have said that there were few nurses who did not give their all to their patients. That some may have done so to a few of the junior doctors out of hospital hours seemed not unlikely, to judge from the tender relationship that seemed to exist between certain of the nurses and certain of the doctors. But this was only surmise on my part, laced with a little envy. As far as the nurses were concerned, they could not have shown greater consideration for their patients than was shown by almost all of them.

There were, however, one or two exceptions. I will not say that Sister Forbes, who was in charge of the Thoracic Ward and consequently in ultimate charge of me, was one of the exceptions; I will only say that on occasion she came as near to being one as made no matter.

She was, I should say, about forty, give or take a charitable year or two, with a rather oversized bust and an equally over-sized sense of her own importance; a good opinion of herself, in fact. It was my guess that she needed this to counteract the opinions of others, which in general were somewhat lower than her own. In conformity with the traditions of St Cyprian's sisters, she wore, perched on the top of her head, a starched cap in the form of a small soufflé dish. It did little for her appearance, which in any case was not particularly prepossessing. There was an air of grim authority about her as she marched along the corridor or through the ward that might well have set back the recovery of a timorous patient by several days, for she seldom deigned to smile, though when she did, the effect was, if anything, more intimidating than were her features when in repose. It was not exactly a fiendish grin, but gave one the sort of uncomfortable feeling that a guest at her table might have experienced when smiled upon by Lucrezia Borgia.

But I must in fairness qualify this portrait of Sister Forbes. Though it could hardly be said that she was universally popular, she was judged to be fair in her dealings with the nurses and was undoubtedly good at her job. She was also, when need be, gentleness itself. I speak from experience, because in my case the need occurred fairly often, there being so many different focuses of pain and discomfort.

I had my first brush with this formidable dame soon after my journey across the Styx had been interrupted, through the intervention of Mr Dring, and I had been unexpectedly pulled back to the shore whence I had set out. Sister Forbes had breezed into my room, as she did from time to time, not with any fixed purpose, except to satisfy herself that everything was shipshape. She was inevitably a great stickler for order and tidiness.

It was while I was having what was jocularly referred to as my lunch that she chose to make her tour of inspection. It was apparent, after she had paused for a few moments to glance at my nasal drip, that she didn't like the look of it. Nor did I, but then I had no choice; but for once my liquid luncheon was finding its way to my alimentary tract without interruption. And God knows, I needed it. I had not at this stage lost the full two stone that fell away during the course of my ordeal, but I must have been near to rock bottom at the time.

I begged the stupid woman to leave things alone, not to fiddle with the apparatus and to let me get what little enjoyment was to be had from the sensation of a vegetable purée trickling down the back of my nose. But she would have none of it. She could see, she said – with what truth, I don't know, as the head of the apparatus was out of my line of sight – that an air-lock was about to interrupt my supply of nutriment. An ill-timed jest, I thought. All went well for a few minutes, then suddenly I felt the supply beginning to fluctuate.

'For God's sake!' I implored her.

'Don't you swear at me,' she said sharply and, I thought, a little illogically.

'As if I would,' I said. 'I was invoking the name of the Lord, that's all.'

'Well, understand: I won't be spoken to like that.'

'But my dear Sister,' I said, 'I was speaking to the Almighty, not to you.' As soon as I said it, I saw that she might take this as an oblique reference to herself. But she let it go. She was intent on her other tack.

'Well, I won't have you talk to me like that.'

'Like *what*?' The woman was obviously insane.

'You know like what.'

'Me no like what, but me likee velly much vegetebu plullée,' I said plaintively, in an endeavour to smooth things over. 'Only now it's not coming through any longer.'

The silly bitch had managed finally to cut off my supply.

'You're trying to starve me into submission,' I said. 'I see it all now. God, this is worse than Treblinka.'

'You know what's the matter with you, don't you?' she said sourly.

'A ruptured oesophagus, collapsed lung, suspected duodenal ulcer, piles: you name it, I've got it,' I said.

She didn't see the joke.

'Look, will you please restore the supply of nutriment to my nose,' I said.

She had nothing to say. Instead, she went on fiddling with my feeding tube.

'Look, why don't you just leave it alone for a few minutes?' I said. 'Perhaps it'll start again of its own accord. I expect it's temperamental, like the rest of us.'

'Temperamental!' she said scathingly. She wasn't to be mollified.

'All I want, Sister, is for you to restore unto me that which is mine. Or was until you started tinkering about.'

'What d'you think I'm trying to do?' She sounded decidedly aggressive.

'I wish I knew,' I said, possibly with the faintest touch of reciprocal asperity. I was beginning to feel a bit fed up by this time, and wishing it were in more than the metaphorical sense.

'There's no need to take that tone,' she said.

'What tone?' I asked, with an air of infuriating innocence. 'My tone is as the dulcimer.'

'You know very well what tone. And if I have any more trouble from you, Mr Dring is going to hear about it.'

'And if you don't lubricate my nose pretty quickly, he'll hear about that, too,' I said. 'My drip-feed was working a treat till you came in and started messing about with it. What have I done to deserve this of you? Don't you love me any more?'

If looks could kill, in my enfeebled state I should have been a goner there and then.

Suddenly there was a return of vegetable purée to my nasal passage.

'Hullo, you've got it going again,' I said. 'How did you manage that?'

'I have operated a drip-feed before, you know.'

'Well, congratulations. Oh, worker of miracles, oh, bringer of balm!'

She snorted. 'You know where you'll end up, if you aren't careful, don't you?' she said. 'In Psychiatric, that's where.'

The All-Seeing Eye

Much of the life of a thoracic patient is spent in being X-rayed. At first, while I was too enfeebled to move or be moved, a gigantic X-ray apparatus was wheeled into my room every morning, its entrance being effected by the opening of the double doors to their fullest extent. I would then be propped up like a scarecrow, to which my generally disordered appearance bore a striking likeness, while cunning snaps of my interior were taken by the radiologist. More often than not the radiologist, I am glad to say, was a young woman. Not always the same young woman, but invariably one of pleasing appearance. I remember one dusky charmer, pretty as a peach, whose attractions were such that her visits, instead of contributing to my recovery, so excited my nervous system that I always felt rather worse than better after she had taken my picture.

At a later stage, as my condition improved, I was placed in a wheel-chair and pushed along the corridors for a mile or so to the X-ray department to be photographed there. On these expeditions

I was often attended by Lionel, one of the hospital porters. He was a stocky youth with a cape of corn-coloured hair that fell from the crown of his head to his elbows. He wore, as a rule, a brightly coloured shirt with a pattern of flowers on it, bell-bottomed denims of spectacular width, and bulbous-toed shoes of two-tone (green and orange) glacé plastic with platform soles. He also wore a short white jacket, such as hospital porters usually wear, only his was several sizes too small and so tight under the arms that his stance was like that of an all-in wrestler going in for the kill. This, I am sure, belied his nature, which appeared to be friendly, so far as could be judged from his conversation, but as this seemed to consist of one word only – 'Right', it was difficult to tell whether in fact he was as benign as his somewhat vacuous expression suggested. His limited command of language was offset, however, by the variety of emphasis that he placed on his solitary adverb. This he could utter in two distinct tones, one indicative of agreement, the other interrogatory.

Having transported me safely to the X-ray department, he would leave me in the passage, there to await the radiologist's pleasure. Others in better or worse shape than myself – it was difficult to tell, as they were usually enveloped in hospital dressing gowns – were sometimes wheeled up to keep me company. Though in their case the spirit appeared willing, it was usually the flesh that seemed weak. Most of them could barely croak, but

64

Lionel

this did not prevent them, if left alone alongside my chair, from trying to strike up an unwanted acquaintance.

I have long subscribed to the belief that unless you know of something worth saying, or have a warning to give, as, for instance, of scaffolding about to fall, or dog's mess on the pavement, the wisest plan is to keep your trap shut. This dictum seemed to be a thing unknown to most of the other X-ray patients. Fatuities about the weather; about the approach of Christmas; about a meal just consumed or one about to be eaten, went winging their way up and down the passage like bats in a cave, with as little sense of purpose and making, on me at any rate, an impression no less disagreeable. I steadfastly refused all commerce of this kind, pretending to be either asleep or too ill to pay heed to these ailing windbags.

In due course the radiologist would step into the passage and rescue me from their garrulous assaults by pushing my chair into the photographic studio. This had less the appearance of a studio than the floor of a factory engaged in the production of heavy armaments, where the workers, all but one, seemed to have gone home for the week-end. Everywhere there were huge machines, work benches no less enormous, and banks of apparatus covered with dials, tubes, lights and levers. And master-minding all of this was usually a maiden of such tender years that you wondered how she could possibly have found time since leaving school to learn the innumerable mysteries of radiology.

Most of the young women in charge were rather severe in manner, as though they expected to be taken advantage of and were determined to make it plain that there was nothing doing; a precaution that seemed superfluous, since most of the male patients needing X-rays seemed to be geriatrics with grave pulmonary troubles. Enfeebled though I was, and encumbered by my jar, and though I needed assistance to get in and out of my chair, as well as support while being X-rayed, I seemed nevertheless to be physically in the pink of condition compared with most of the others. It was, in fact, rather heartening to see how spry were my movements, how alert my reactions, in comparison with theirs.

There are two different ways, it seems, of X-raying the thorax. In one, my photograph was taken in a somewhat unusual pose: stripped to the waist and shivering, I stood against a metal frame, to which with arms outstretched and face averted, I clung, as if awaiting the dreaded swish of a cat-o'-nine-tails. The radiologist meanwhile peered intently into a monitor in which the secrets of the X-ray were revealed, as on a TV screen. No matter how sensational these effects might be, she remained totally impassive, so that there was no guessing at the possible significance of the pictures she had taken. I longed for the proceedings to be enlivened by a start of surprise, a low, incredulous whistle, or even a burst of laughter, but no: decorum remained the order of the day.

The other procedure, invoked as my condition improved, was rather more complicated. First, I was required to squeeze into a neatly constructed aperture in an enormous machine that looked like a horizontal printing press, and then over the barrier thus formed, which separated me from the outside world, I was handed a strawberry yoghourt. Then, on the word of command from the fair radiologist, I took a mouthful of the stuff, swilled it round, and swallowed it as directed. This procedure I repeated several times, turning my body the while from left to right and then from right to left. I thought at first this was to give the girl a glimpse of my profile and felt somewhat abashed to find that her interest was only in my duodenum. Finally, the count-down for take off would begin and bracing myself for what was to follow, I would lean back against the interior wall of the machine while the whole vast apparatus began to perform a slow parabola, coming to a halt as soon as my body had reached a horizontal position.

When enough snaps had been taken of my stomach from this angle, I would brace myself once more, this time for the return to earth, and the machine, operating in reverse, would eventually restore me to the perpendicular. Flushed with the pride of achievement and the flatulence resulting from the revolution given to my intestines, I would step forth, flop back into my chair, and

68

clutching my jar between my knees, would be wheeled back by Lionel to the ward.

As a ministering angel, Lionel was invariably polite and solicitous, never failing to envelop my form in a blanket before we set off on our trips to or from the hinterland, so that the northerly blasts which swept through the main corridor at gale force should be mitigated. Only once did his consideration for me as a patient lapse. On the return journey we were somewhat less than half-way along the corridor, through which the wind was whistling like a demented shepherd seeking a lost sheepdog, when Lionel was hailed by a friend, who was pushing a trolley laden with pillows and blankets. He was a lanky youth and was dressed in gear much the same as Lionel's, but with the addition of a knee-length necklace and a pair of high-heeled Mexican boots. His hair he wore in the fashionable Afro style, so that his weazened face peeped out from beneath a ball of fuzz some two feet in diameter. He was clearly well acquainted with Lionel's linguistic handicap because his conversation was so directed that no other response was needed than the solitary word of which Lionel had such eloquent command. His babbling was of discos and motor cycles, and for some ten minutes, while I crouched shivering in my chair, his oratory poured forth, with an occasional interruption ('Right . . . right! . . . right?') from Lionel. At length, with my teeth chattering like castanets, I ventured to suggest that we might push on.

'Right,' said Lionel.

His friend saluted him with a vigorous punch on the shoulder.

'Well, I better piss off. See yuh.'

'Right,' said Lionel, and we went on our way.

By this stage of the game I was able, though not without the darkest apprehensions and some hideous grimacing, to hoist myself from my wheelchair back into bed. On this occasion, Lionel, sensing that disaster might be imminent, stepped forward to lend me a hand. But with that iron determination that can only be overcome by a word from my wife ('Don't you dare!'), I waved away his proffered assistance.

'Okay, I can manage, thanks.'

'Right,' said Lionel.

Day by Day

All good things must come to an end, and after several weeks it was decided that my nasal drip should be removed. Thereafter, by gradual degrees, I reverted to a normal diet. Did I say normal diet? I should have said National Health hospital fodder. Let me give you a resumé of the way in which my days were spent thereafter:

AM

6.30

Reveille; followed by a perfunctory scrub down by one of the night staff, eager to return to the ward pantry for a nice cup of tea.

6.35–8.00

Sit up in bed, staring vacantly into space, too sleepy to read, not sleepy enough to drop off again.

8.00

Breakfast: cereal or porridge (this looked too like the contents of my jar to be appetizing); lightly boiled egg (which I detest); sausage and bacon and/or bacon and sausage; bread and butter (?), jam or marmalade; coffee (very weak) or PG Tips (very, *very* strong). Pills.

8.30

Injection; followed by bed-bath; not very enjoyable even at the tender hands of Susie and Yvonne.

9.00

Bundled into armchair by the window, there to spend the rest of the day. (Oh, God!)

9.15

Inspection by Mr Dring, accompanied by Sister. This occasion was sometimes used for giving a short lecture about my case to other members of the Thoracic staff. My X-rays would be exhibited, while I, like some prize specimen of cattle, would be shown off to the awe-struck gathering, emphasis being laid on the finer points of my anatomy (*ie*, where my bones, though not actually protruding through the flesh, were too near the surface for comfort). Though I usually understood not a word of what Mr Dring was talking about, it seemed to go down well with his audience, which would occasionally titter at some physiological witticism or gasp in wonder, as if to express astonishment at my survival. (I don't mind telling you, I was astonished at it myself.)

9.30

Elevenses, followed by injection.

Lecture tour

12.15

Luncheon. I won't bore you with the menu, which was, indeed, excruciatingly boring.

1.15

Injection.

2.15

Five o'clock tea.

4.00

Arrival of morning newspaper.

6.15

Injection.

6.30

Retire to bed, utterly worn out.

7.00

Dinner (ugh!)

8.00

Drop off, after struggle to keep awake.

8.30

Awoken by noisy arrival of night staff.

9.30

Bed-bath by auxiliary nurse, somewhat out of training for this sort of caper, followed by final injection of the day.

10.00

Settle down to sleep.

10.30

Awoken by conscientious auxiliary to see if there is anything I want. ('Yes,' I say, 'I want to get some *sleep*!').

11.30

Unable to drop off after previous interruption, I ring and ask for sleeping pills.

12.00

Auxiliary brings pills and wishes me goodnight 'and sweet dreams' (silly cow!).

Gladys

Gladys was the lady who came every day to clean my room. Though at first, in the extremity of my illness, I was no more than dimly aware of a shuffling form moving about, as I became more conscious of my surroundings and of those by whom my days were peopled, I realized that Gladys was a creature of flesh and blood. There was plenty of flesh, but the pallor of her face, enhanced by a thick patina of rice powder, suggested that the blood must have been rather scarce. Her invariable get-up comprised a dainty flowered overall, rubber gloves, felt slippers of enormous size, and a turban, worn rather low down on her forehead, so that from the back of it there protruded a ragged fringe of hair, richly hennaed. That the henna had not been applied for some time was apparent from its colour having faded almost to that of a blush rose, adding to her appearance a touch of surprise for those who, having seen the front view, might walk round to see what the back was like.

There are some people who are never so happy

as when they are miserable. Gladys was one of these. Her life seemed to have been invaded by sorrows since her childhood, nor had they deserted her yet. Misfortunes of every kind had rained upon her. She had had a close acquaintance with injury, sickness and death; with mental illness and suicide; with rising damp, dry rot, theft, burglary, fire and flood. There seemed to be few disasters of the type to which man is prone that she had not suffered at one time or another, if not directly as a victim, then vicariously through the agency of her family or friends. At first I felt deeply sympathetic towards her, but as one disaster piled itself upon another in her conversation, and as after each one, she seemed to come up smiling, as it were, in anticipation of the next, I began to temper my sympathy with reserve. I wasn't feeling too fit myself and would have preferred to hear a few glad tidings from her now and again, but none were forthcoming.

She was still grieving, after eighteen years, for the loss of her eldest son, who, it subsequently transpired on her own admission, was not dead at all, but hale and hearty, a sergeant in the Royal Marines and a happily married man with three children. It sounded as though he was a good and affectionate son, but his leaving the nest, though it had happened so long ago, had been a blow from which Gladys clearly hoped never to recover. Her younger son had had TB, but had been cured, leaving her permanently resentful at having been cheated of yet another sorrow. And when, after falling out of a tree and breaking her back, her daughter Sharon had made a perfect recovery, it must have seemed almost as though there was a conspiracy to deprive poor Gladys of those disasters that did so much to sustain her morale.

Bedridden as I was, there was no escaping the litany of her woes. All I could do was to pretend to be asleep. But she soon rumbled me, and thereafter would contrive, either by dropping something on the floor with a crash or bumping the bed as if by accident with her floor polishing equipment, to wake me up with a start. It was useless then to pretend to drop off again. In any case, the flicker of an eyelid would set her off at once.

''member I told you about my friend Mrs Blake? Poor thing, do you know what? Her sister's friend's nephew's gone and fallen down and cracked his pelvis. I said to her . . .'

At such moments, even the appearance of Sister Forbes, with hypodermic at the ready, would come as a relief.

From Outer Space

It was not until after I had been in St Cyprian's for about two weeks that I was allowed to see visitors; apart from Madeleine, that is, who had loyally driven thirty miles a day to sit beside my bed for an hour or two, while I lay comfortably snoozing, and then had driven thirty miles back again. Even when I became less comatose and was able to sit up and embark on an endless series of complaints, these visits can hardly have been, for her, less rewarding. At first, more often than not, my face would be buried in an oxygen mask. It is not easy under such a handicap to convey one's feelings, but I did try, with various winks and grimaces, to show her how much I appreciated her presence. She told me later on that she had assumed these efforts to be merely a sign of acute indigestion; a recurrence in fact of the belching syndrome.

As generous as she was patient, Madeleine invariably came bearing gifts. Food I could not eat, but she brought me flowers, refreshing lotions, playing cards, against the day when I might again feel equal to the emotional hurly-burly of a game of Miss Milligan, and out-of-date copies of *The Economist*. In one of these was reported at some length an absolutely thrilling speech that had been delivered some three weeks previously by Mr Douglas Jay to a select gathering of Trade Unionists. I do not say that the excitement engendered by this had anything to do with my relapse; it may be no more than a coincidence but, having read it, I did suffer a slight set-back. Thereafter, on the advice of Mr Dring, such heady stuff was banned from the sick-room. Truth to tell, though *The Economist* was meat and drink to Madeleine – was indeed her Bible and a potent source of intellectual inspiration, I seldom felt as famished for lack of its stimulus as did she, if ever the week's issue failed to be delivered. I rather preferred to have a look at *Penthouse*.

I did not like to tell her myself that I was no longer to be allowed to peruse the sacred pages of her favourite journal; she might have argued me out of it, and I didn't want that. So I persuaded Mr Dring to break the news to her.

She took it bravely and on her next visit brought me instead a copy of *House and Garden*. It did not take me long to come to the conclusion that *The Economist* would be preferable. I have never myself gone in for gracious living. Perhaps I lack the sophistication that you need to make a success of it, or lack perhaps the ability to decide which type of indoor greenery will be best suited to the muted elegance of a Chinese wallpaper. Nor am I at my best lounging beside a heated swimming pool with a long, cool glass of bacardi in my fist and by my side a model in a bikini with a look of studied vacancy on her smooth oiled face, as innocent of make-up as Mother Teresa's. And while I like my scoff, I am not sufficiently a judge of food or drink to speak with conviction of the merits of *Crème de Poissons au Cari* over Creole Crab Gumbo, or of a Chateau Latour '71 over a Mouton Rothschild '73. And what's more, I don't care; though as time went on, I must confess to a feeling that Creole Crab Gumbo might be preferable to National Health fish-pie.

In addition to Madeleine's daily visits, I later began to have visits from all manner of well-wishers, unsuspicious of my preference for solitude when feeling slightly out of sorts. But they, too, were so kind and generous, appearing laden with flowers and fruit, with clotted cream and bottles of brandy and Penguin paperbacks, that I hadn't the heart to repel them. Besides, I needed the brandy, and Madeleine, I need hardly say, made short work of the clotted cream.

First to appear at my bedside was Mrs Walsingham, an elderly neighbour of benevolent disposition and statuesque proportions. She reminded both of us, Madeleine and me, of Henry VIII. We had often commented on this resemblance, and in her flat, black, feathered toque, and with her small eyes and still smaller mouth embedded in a large fleshy face, she could, I am sure, have gone *au nature* to a fancy dress ball and easily have won First Prize as Bluff King Hal.

I was asleep when she arrived. It was 2.15 p.m. and afternoon tea was about to be served, so Susie, thinking that probably I would soon wake up and call for char and crumpets, had mistakenly given the widow Walsingham a chair beside my bed. When I awoke, I imagined at first that I must still be dreaming, for my dreams had been for some reason or other about elephants. The sight of Mrs Walsingham sitting so close at hand, reading a dog-eared copy of *The Economist* picked up off my bedside table, seemed such an utter impossibility, a turn of fantasy so ludicrous, that I could not believe my eyes. I stared at her blindly for a second or two then pulled up the bedclothes round my ears and prepared to drop off again. But there was something in that too, too solid flesh, that all too familiar toque with its sable plume, that suddenly gave me to think again. Was this an apparition of Mrs Walsingham, or Mrs Walsingham *in veritas*?

I took a peek at her from underneath the blankets, then quickly closed my eyes again. There could be no doubt about it: she was a reality.

She had brought with her a sickly-looking cyclamen of an even sicklier shade of mauve. This she had placed upon my bedside table, that it might rest in my line of vision the moment I awoke. So there it was. I decided immediately to give it later on to the night sister. It was important to keep in her good books; besides, this anaemic-looking bloom seemed exactly suited to her personality.

'Mrs Walsingham,' I said, 'how very good of you to come and see me. And what a perfectly beautiful cyclamen! You are kind.'

She gave a deprecating smile, then after a brief word of commiseration, launched out into a stream of recollections about her own experiences in hospital. These had been many and various: tonsillitis in childhood, bronchial troubles in adolescence, and since then, gallstones, appendicitis, the removal of a cartilage, a hiatus hernia and a hysterectomy. Not counting the last, I felt that all things considered I seemed to have got off pretty lightly.

This recital of Mrs Walsingham's health problems and cognate matters lasted until it was time for her to go, when she rose up and taking my hand, said, 'Well, what a time you've had. I expect you've been glad to have someone to pour it all out to.'

There is no occasion like being in hospital for bringing home to one the true worth of one's neighbours. Mine rallied round my sick-bed with a touching pertinacity that I could well have done without. Another who came to see me was Roderick Rumbold. I did not know him well, nor did I want to, for although he was much esteemed for his conscientious activities in the social life of the county, a pillar of the local preservation society, president of our local music group, and a keen amateur archaeologist, he was one of the most colossal bores it has ever been my bad luck to be saddled with. From the crown of his tweed hat to the soles of his well-worn suede shoes, he reeked of complacency. For an hour, until I pretended to feel faint, he gave me a blow by blow account of his tedious, well-intentioned doings, telling me all about his bold confrontation of various local interests who were opposed to his own, and of how he had worsted all of them single-handed.

'I knew you'd be interested,' he said, as he got up to go. 'One does feel so isolated in hospital.'

'Well, to tell you the truth,' I said, 'it's been rather a pleasant rest.'

'But I expect you'll be glad to get back into the swing again? How long do you intend to stay here?'

It was too good an opening. 'As long as possible,' I said.

Another of my visitors was a lady whom we had got to know only quite recently, a Mrs Carey-Wilson. We were having drinks one Sunday morning with some friends when our hostess, in what I can only assume was a moment of total amnesia, dragged this wretched woman up and introduced us to her. Well, you know how you can sometimes tell straight away when you're introduced to someone whether you're going to get on with them or not: the briefest glimpse at Mrs Carey-Wilson was enough. To start with, anyone who goes out to drinks on a Sunday morning wearing a *hat* shouldn't even be admitted to the house. However, there she was this ghastly woman, wearing a hat that looked like summer pudding on which someone had started to sit down. One look at it, and I knew I wanted no part of Mrs Carey-Wilson. In fact, the very thought of the different parts of her that might otherwise have been accessible to me made me feel quite queasy. So as soon as I decently could, I edged myself away and started talking to the vicar; anything, I thought, would be better than having to make conversation to such a threat to one's peace of mind as Mrs Carey-Wilson represented.

Madeleine, who has no such inhibitions about bores as I have, stood her ground and I daresay gave as good as she got. On the way home she told me something of what had been said. Mrs Carey-Wilson, it seemed, had only recently moved into the neighbourhood. I asked Madeleine if she had said how soon she was moving out again, but on this point she had vouchsafed nothing. And now she had moved in beside my bed, and I could see she was going to be difficult to get rid of. However, at the end of fifteen minutes I had a brain-wave and I reached up and rang my bell.

Mrs Carey-Wilson prattled on until the door opened and Jean appeared.

'Jean,' I said, 'could I have a bed-pan, please';

then to Mrs Carey-Wilson: 'I'm terribly sorry; but this is nature's doing, not mine . . .'

I am happy to say that from that day to this we have seen neither hide nor hair, nor even hat, of Mrs Carey-Wilson.

Mango Chutney

From time to time I had noticed and been faintly puzzled by a handsome Indian, who now and then appeared in the corridor or the ward. He had about him an air of abstraction that suggested that there was much on his mind, as though perhaps he were weighing the *pros* and *cons* of the latest move by Mrs Gandhi or was suffering from a surfeit of prawn curry. I put him down as being somewhere about thirty and presumably a member of the staff, since he wore a white coat. Clearly, he was not a doctor; his coat was short, like my monosyllabic friend Lionel's, and with it he wore a blue arm-band. I had also encountered him once or twice on my way to or from X-rays and had noticed then the stately way in which he walked, placing his feet on the ground with a deliberation that suggested he had thought carefully about the wisdom and possible consequences of doing so. The same deliberation marked the retraction of the foot from the ground, so that his progress resembled the leisurely advance of a whooping crane. And I had noticed another thing: that both patients and nurses addressed him by the unlikely nickname of 'Marmalade'.

One day, a week or so before Christmas, my door was opened – for once someone had shut it – and Marmalade looked in. Seeing me sitting like a shrivelled patriarch in my armchair by the window, he bowed and pressed his palms together in salute.

'May I enter?'

It was the first time I had heard him speak and he did so in soft, melodious tones that matched the habitual gravity of his appearance.

'Of course,' I said, putting down the copy of *Playboy* that I had been glancing at. 'Please come in.'

He advanced a little way into the room and stopped at the bottom of the bed, fingering the clip-board that held my charts and which hung from the bed-rail. His blue-black hair and the pallor of his translucent skin dramatized his sensational good looks, to which there was only one impediment; he had a faint squint. It was as if he was trying to focus on the space between his eyebrows.

He stood there, smiling shyly at me. Nothing further was said; nor, as the seconds ticked by, seemed likely to be. I felt it incumbent on me, therefore, to push the boat out.

'What can I do for you?' I asked. It seemed a safe, non-controversial opening.

'Ah, yes, indeed.' Again he paused. 'This is a

very nice room you have,' he said, looking about my minute chamber as though it were an apartment in some stately home. 'The grass is to be seen from the window.'

I could see he was one of those gifted with utterance of the self-evident.

'Yes, it's not exactly a splendid view, but it helps.'

'It helps?'

'It's better than looking out on a slag heap.'

'Excuse me, but what is slag heap?'

'A rubbish heap.'

'Ah, yes. Rubbish.'

This seemed to provide him with food for thought; a good solid meal, in fact, for another long silence followed. I felt we were not getting anywhere, and having no idea which direction we were supposed to be taking, I decided to chance my arm and strike off at a tangent.

'Tell me, I've often seen you about, but you know I have no idea what you do.'

'I do many things,' said Marmalade cryptically.

'Yes, but I mean here, in the hospital.'

'Here in the hospital? I am nurse.'

'Ah, a male nurse.'

'That is correct. I am most definitely not a female nurse.' This was said without so much as the ghost of a smile.

'But you are not on the ward?'

'I am not on this ward, Thoracic Ward. I am summoned from time to time when there is staff shortage and I am able to be spared from my own ward.'

'And which ward is that?' I asked.

'I am in Amputation Ward. It is very, very interesting. Much more interesting than Thoracic Ward.'

I felt slightly put down.

'Well then, tell me another thing.' A look of polite inquiry spread itself over Marmalade's exquisite features. 'Perhaps I shouldn't ask, but I've often wondered; why do they call you Marmalade?'

'Because my name is Jam,' said Marmalade gravely, leaving me to work out for myself the logic of the proposition.

'I apologise for the British sense of humour,' I said.

'It is very peculiar, I think.'

'You can say *that* again.'

'It is very peculiar, I think.'

'I think so too.'

'But you yourself are British?'

'But I don't have their sense of humour.'

'How is that possible?'

I felt we were getting into waters where I might easily drown, having little appetite and less strength for philosophical argument.

'Well, it's possible, I suppose, because I'm a Scotsman.'

'Ah.' He seemed, as I intended, him to be, completely baffled.

'I must say, I prefer Jam,' I said.

'Do you, yes? I think marmalade is good though. We do not make a lot of marmalade in India, you see. But we make much mango chutney.'

'Yes, I suppose you do.'

'Oh yes, indeed. It is very, very good. Have you ever tasted mango chutney?'

'I've tried it.'

He discerned in a trice what I thought of mango chutney, and his eyes filled with tears.

'You don't like mango chutney?'

'It's all right,' I said, hoping to cheer him up by an effort of compromise.

'I'm sorry you don't like it – very, very sorry indeed.' He looked down at my bedclothes and shook his head mournfully.

'It's just a matter of taste,' I said.

He considered this for a moment.

'I see. You are quite right: a matter of taste.' He began to brighten visibly. 'You are liking jam; I am liking mango chutney. A matter of taste. That is very, very good.'

The pearl of wisdom that appeared to have dropped from my lips seemed to have acted as a restorative.

'But I must not stand here and chatter. Otherwise we shall be here all day.'

'No hurry,' I said, and immediately repented of it.

'Oh, yes, yes. I must not waste your valuable

time. You have some serious reading to do, I can see that, you see.'

'No, no, I was only just looking at a magazine,' I said, trying to shuffle *Playboy* underneath the mattress, as though that were where I normally kept my reading matter. 'You haven't told me, by the way, what it is you want of me.'

'Yes, I must disclose the purpose of my visit. No one has told you?'

'No one tells me anything,' I said.

He paused again, then cleared his throat. 'I have come to give you a bath.'

'A bath? Good God!'

'I am very, very sorry to give you such a bad shock.' His tone was more than solicitous; it was deeply sympathetic. 'I can see you are shocked, you see.'

'Not shocked. Surprised, though. I haven't had a bath – I mean not a proper bath – since I've been here.'

'Thus it is necessary you should have a bath now, you see.'

I did see. Probably I was smelling like a skunk and no one had liked to tell me so.

'Where is the bathroom?'

'At the end of the corridor, not far.'

'And what do I do about this damned jar?' I asked. I was still attached to my incubus.

'Oh, that will be quite all right. You bring your damn jar with you.'

I heaved myself out of my armchair, got a grip on my jar and went trailing after Jam along the corridor.

The idea of having a bath, a proper bath in a tub with taps and a bath mat on the floor, instead of the blanket substitute that I had got used to being given by Sally or Sandra, had haunted me like vision, like a dream. Lying in bed or sitting in my chair, tears had sprung to my eyes at the thought of sponge and flannel. I had meditated sadly on the unattainable loofah. And now, all of a sudden, the dream had come true. Here I was, sitting waist-high in warm water, with my tube trailing over the side of the bath and Jam acting as nanny. Very gently, he soaped and sluiced me all over and topped off the proceedings by giving me a shampoo.

When it was all over, I emerged from the bathroom feeling a new man, bearing my jar boldly and footing it along the corridor with a firm tread. Jam escorted me back to my room and waited to see me ensconced once more in my chair by the window.

'Thank you, Jam,' I said. 'That was a great experience. I feel thoroughly rejuvenated.'

'You are most welcome.'

My tea tray had been brought in during our absence and on it were two horrible little slices of Dundee cake.

'Would you like a cup of tea?' I said.

'No, thank you, no tea.'

I noticed that Jam was staring covetously at the cake.

'A piece of cake, then?'

'That is very, very kind.'

A chameleon with its prehensile tongue could not have latched onto a fly with greater speed than Jam pounced on the smaller of the two slices.

'Have 'em both,' I said, holding the plate out to him. 'I never eat cake; not this sort anyway.'

'Very well, if you insist.'

In a second the larger slice had followed the smaller. Jam's cheeks looked as if they would burst.

'It is very, very good cake,' he said in tones heavily muffled, spewing crumbs onto the bed-cover in a neat semi-circle.

'Glad you like it.'

There then ensued an even longer silence than before, not this time because Jam was cogitating, but because speech was an impossibility.

'I'm sorry about the mango chutney,' I said at length. I felt I couldn't just write off a matter that was so close to his heart without some sort of apology for having wounded his feelings, even though unintentionally.

With a final gulp that seemed to send his adam's apple into the roof of his mouth, he disposed of the last mouthful of cake.

'Yes, but as you have observed so very, very wisely, it is a matter of taste, you see.'

He pressed his palms together in front of him, bowed, and backed out of the room.

I vowed that, cost me what it might, at home once more I would make a last supreme effort to enjoy mango chutney.

Physical Jerks

Came the day when I was considered to be ripe for the physiotherapist. At St Cyprian's the 'physios' seemed always to go about in pairs, like the women police and with the same air of leisurely unconcern, as though they were on the beat. They were dressed like magpies in an elegant outfit of black and white and seemed a conspiciously attractive bunch of girls, until they got their hands on you.

I remember – shall I ever forget? – the day of Christine's first visit. Christine was tall and good-looking. To my regret, she always wore dark glasses, or more precisely, glasses that were tinted, so that you could just see her eyes, but not their expression, which I guessed was for the most part one of cool amusement. I asked her one day whether she wore them for opthalmic reasons or to hide from herself the pain she inflicted on her patients.

'On the contrary,' she said. 'It's for the pain they inflict on me. Have you ever had a look at them out there, that bunch in Thoracic?'

I could see her point. Stumbling about the ward

with my jam jar, I had had plenty of opportunity to observe the patients and would have said that by and large there were often more attractive specimens to be seen in our local cattle market.

Before Christine's first appearance I had been put through a few preliminary hoops under the gentle tuition of Sister Forbes and Sally. They had come into my room one morning and had stood at the bottom of the bed, smiling at me with a look that I couldn't quite make out.

'Guess what we're going to do,' said Sally.

'I give up,' I said.

'We're going for a walk,' said Sister Forbes.

I looked out of the window. It was pouring with rain.

'But you'll both get soaked,' I said.

'Oh, no, we won't,' said Sally.

'How so?' I asked, little thinking what was to follow.

'Because you're coming with us,' said Sister Forbes, and as she spoke she whipped aside my bedclothes like a conjuror whisking away a table-cloth.

'You must be out of your minds!' I screamed.

'No nonsense,' Forbes riposted, and before I knew where I was, she had grasped me by the ankles and swung me round on my bottom, so that my legs dangled over the edge of the bed.

I appealed to Sally.

'I thought you were my friend.'

'Well, now you know better, don't you?' she

said, clamping off my rubber tube, so as to be able to effect a severance between me and my jam jar. 'Come on, love, take my arm.'

And so, supported by Sally on one side and Sister Forbes on the other, I was dragged out into the corridor, where they hauled me slowly up and down.

'Now try walking,' said Sister Forbes, after a few minutes. Her support for my helpless form slackened a little.

'Come on, try,' said Sally.

'Anything to oblige,' I said. I did as requested and went down flat on my face.

'You pushed me,' I said to Sister Forbes, as she helped me up.

'That's a lie, I never touched you.'

'Have another go,' said Sally.

I didn't mind whether I was in Sister Forbes's good graces or not, but Sally's opinion of me was a different matter. I braced myself for another attempt.

At the end of ten minutes I was managing to put one foot tentatively in front of the other without keeling over.

'That's great!' said Sally.

I repeated the process for another few yards, then sank slowly to the ground. Again Sister Forbes yanked me to my feet.

'What's the matter? You been drinking or something?'

At this moment O'Grady appeared.

'Don't let her bully you, love, give her a kick,' she said.

'Don't be funny,' I said. 'It's all I can do to stand on two legs, let alone one.'

'Ahr, she's a real divil, that Forbes, ain't she?' she said sympathetically.

'Clear off!' said Sister Forbes.

'Pay her no heed,' said O'Grady. 'You just lie on the floor, if that's what you want.'

'You're a subversive influence, that's what you are,' said Sister Forbes.

'And if I weren't on duty,' said O'Grady, 'I'd give you one in the kisser.'

The continuation of this ugly outburst was prevented only by the emergence from the ward of Dr Robertshaw.

'So Hamlet's father walks again,' he said gravely and disappeared along the corridor.

He was followed from the ward a moment later by Mr Dring. Seeing my wilting form supported on either side, he waved cheerily, exclaiming as he passed, 'Haven't forgotten we're playing Cheltenham on Friday, have you? I've put you down for scrum half.'

I was in no mood for such ribaldry. It was all I could do to stagger, with Sally's support, as far as my room, where I climbed back into bed, exhausted. For three or four days running this grisly farce was repeated. By that time I was thought to be in a fit condition to face up to Christine.

You wouldn't have thought that a girl who looked so attractive and so gentle would be capable of acts of such bestial ferocity as Christine committed against my person during the time that I was her helpless victim. Acts comparatively painless culminated a few weeks later in tortures of unimaginable cruelty. To begin with, we did simple breathing exercises. That is to say, I did the breathing and she did the exercises, forcing my torpid lungs in and out by manual pressure. When in the course of this operation enough phlegm had accumulated in my throat, I expectorated daintily into a plastic cup, which was afterwards sent to the laboratory for analysis. I can think of few more uncongenial ways of passing the time than analysing the sputum of a total stranger. At least some trace of fellow-feeling might be expected to enter into the analysis of what a near and dear relative might cough up – one's aunt, say, or one's grandmother – but how can analytical fervour be generated by totally anonymous phlegm? I put the question to Christine.

'I wouldn't bother your head about that,' she said. 'Just keep spitting.'

From breathing exercises we moved on to the task of restoring operational control of those muscles that had atrophied through my lying so long in bed. Although the rack was invented for a different purpose, its effect must have been much the same as that of Christine's efforts to improve the tone of my muscular system. She went about

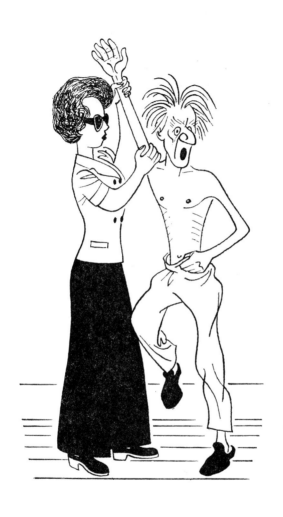

Speeding the patient's recovery

her task with an air of calm that seemed to suggest that she was either indifferent to my sufferings or was taking a secret sadistic delight in inflicting them.

My right arm, which by this time looked like a stick of celery, only less appetizing, being pocked from wrist to elbow with the marks of hypodermics, had grown so stiff at the shoulder that you would have thought there was nothing for it but to break it off. Christine obviously thought so too, and it was not for want of trying that she failed to do so. My legs also had withered till they looked like a pair of crutches. The remedy, though, was not to break them off, but to pound them till they fell off. How fervently I wished they would while Christine's iron-clad hands chopped their way up and down my tibia and fibula!

But it would be ungenerous to deny that she was cruel only to be kind. I knew it, but at the time found it hard to believe. Perhaps if I had been able to see what was going on behind those dark glasses, I would have felt better able to grin and bear it.

Oft in the Stilly Night

At St Cyprian's the curfew tolled the knell of part-
ing day at about eight-thirty. It was at this hour that
the changing of the guard took place: the day staff
left and the night staff reported for duty. The exit
of the day staff was frequently accompanied by ill-
suppressed whoops and screams of anticipation, as
visions arose of pleasures yet to come at the disco
or the staff hop, or possibly to follow a candle-lit
meal, *tête à tête* with one of the junior doctors.

The arrival of the night staff was scarcely less
rowdy and was often the occasion for noisy
camaraderie between them and their departing
colleagues. The tonic effect of this nightly encounter
could not fail to be felt by a patient suffering after
a recent operation or under the weather from some
other cause.

The night staff consisted mostly of auxiliaries,
leavened by a sprinkling of sisters, who used to
flit from ward to ward, hypodermic at the ready,
giving a jab here, a jab there, as fancy took them;
or so it seemed to one so long on the receiving end
of their syringes as was I.

Until she came to settle me down for the night, and thereafter until morning, I was tended by Edie, a stout, cheerful lady of some fifty summers, and by Gloria, whose name was something of a misnomer. Such glory as she may once have possessed had left few traces; she was dim, drab and depressed. She had not much to say for herself, which was lucky, for when she did unleash her reluctant tongue the catalogue of her woes eclipsed even that of Gladys the cleaner.

Edie was shaped rather like a barrel; or perhaps a keg would be a more appropriate simile, for she was exceedingly short. Movement in virtually any direction was hampered by her figure and in my small room she could never turn round without bumping into something, usually the bed, causing me to flood the covers with whatever nauseous brew had been prepared for me as a night-cap. Such collisions were invariably accompanied by mock groans or appeals to Jesus. Difficult though it was for her to get about the room, she found the changing of a sheet or blanket even harder. With Susie, Sandra, or even Hopeless Dawn, this would have been accomplished in a flash, but with Edie it was a major operation, owing not only to the shortness of her arms and legs, but also to the shortness of her breath. After any such exertion she would collapse, panting, into the armchair.

'I ought to be where you are,' she would wheeze.

'Righto, climb in,' I said on one occasion, lifting up the sheets by way of invitation.

The paroxysm of asthmatic giggles that greeted this rather feeble sally must have reverberated throughout the ward.

I was never so successful in getting a smile out of Gloria. The most she would yield was usually a blank look and a shake of the head, as though she considered my case to be beyond human aid, even though this prognostication had long since been abandoned by the experts.

You might have supposed that all would be peace and tranquillity in the ward at night, but no. I was not allowed to have my door shut, the theory being that whoever was on duty would be able to tip-toe into my room and see that all was well without waking me up. But as most often it was Edie who tip-toed in – if a pelican, whose gait hers resembled, can be said to walk on tip-toe – and as without fail she managed every time either to jog the bed, or, in turning round, to knock something over, or off the table, this well-intentioned precaution was without much effect. Consequently, with the door open I was able – indeed, could hardly fail – to hear what was happening in the ward.

Sometimes the place echoed with groans and sometimes with sounds of delirium and a more or less regular accompaniment to the hours of darkness was a mixed chorus of coughing, oicking and, especially, breaking of wind. Two or three of the patients seemed to have attained an outstanding skill in this. I say two or three because I cannot conceive that a single individual would be capable of the barrage of sound that frequently echoed from the ward, often calling forth protests or jocular comment from the other patients, as, 'Blow, blow, thou winter wind' or else, 'Cannon to right of them, cannon to left of them, volleyed and thundered.'

I was reminded on one such occasion of an incident that happened at school, which concerned a young crony of mine, MacDuff by name, who, although no more than thirteen or fourteen years old, was discovered later to have a duodenal ulcer. One effect of this was that he was liable to break wind loudly and often; an accomplishment of which he was inordinately proud, as young boys usually are who find themselves the possessor of some unusual gift. Another of the boys – his name, I seem to recollect, was Evans – who was keen on becoming a doctor and was equally keen on practical jokes, suggested to Macduff one day that he should act as a guinea pig to prove a theory held by Evans that certain gases that accumulate in the lower bowel are inflammable. Macduff, a sporting youth, declared his willingness to take part in the experiment, and that night in the dormitory, after lights out, he was given a meal of baked beans and bicarbonate of soda, a mixture which, according to Evans, was bound to produce an accumulation of wind. Some ten minutes after he had finished his repast, MacDuff, declaring a fart to be imminent, exposed his bottom over the end of his bed, while Evans stood by with a lighted taper. The rest of us gathered round the foot of Macduff's bed in eager anticipation. One boy, I remember, a nervous lad, stood with his eyes tight shut and his fingers in his ears.

'Stand by, boys,' said Macduff, 'I'm nearly ready.'

'Ready for what, may I ask?'

As these words were uttered, the lights in the dormitory went on and there in the doorway was Mr Mallory, the housemaster. Macduff, quick as lightning, exchanged his somewhat unusual posture for a squatting position on the end of his bed.

'Would somebody mind telling me what is going on?' said Mr Mallory in a voice of doom, as he advanced into the room. No one seemed inclined to satisfy his curiosity. 'Well?'

'Well, sir . . .' Evans began, then dried up, at a loss to offer a convincing explanation of the curious tableau that Mr Mallory had interrupted. His taper, which was still alight, was within a few inches of Macduff's face, when Macduff, with superb timing, brought off the most terrific belch. There was a flash of blueish-yellow flame which extinguished the taper and sent Mr Mallory staggering back.

'You see,' said Evans, 'I was right.'

It is idle to complain of what one has to put up with in hospital. It is all for one's own good, though I must say I was never able to see what good Sister Holloway did to me. She appeared only at night, and like certain other nocturnal creatures, was rather displeasing. She didn't mean to be, any more than a stoat or a bat; she just couldn't help it. And, come to think of it, she wasn't unlike a bat; she had a twittering manner and huge ears and her vision was distinctly myopic. She would often peek into my room before I settled down for the night and would stand in the doorway, grinning. Sometimes she would sidle across to my bedside table to see what I was reading.

'May I?' she would say playfully, picking up my book and glancing at it to see what it was. On one occasion it was *Fanny Hill*, and I shall always remember with delight her expression as she put it down after her eye had lighted on one of the fruitier passages.

'I tell you who I am *very* fond of,' she said one night. And she put her head on one side and smiled at me winsomely.

'Me?' I said.

'Oh, Mr Bentley, that goes without saying.' And she tittered, flinging herself about in an ecstasy of something or other, I wasn't quite sure what, then straightened up again.

'No, I tell you who it is: Winston Graham.'

I might have known it.

'*Poldark*. Have you ever read any of the Poldark books?'

'Not yet,' I said, making a mental reservation not to do so.

'Oh, he's so – so—'

'Sloppy?' I suggested.

'Ah, you're making fun of me, Mr Bentley.'

'As if I would!'

'Have you a favourite author?' she asked.

'Yes – me,' I said.

Again she tittered, teetering.

'I *must* read one your books.'

'I'll send you one,' I said.

'Would you really? Oh, how wonderful that would be! May I ask which one?'

'*Gone with the Wind*,' I said. 'I write under a pseudonym.'

'Mr Bentley, you're hopeless,' she said, 'quite hopeless.' She sighed prodigiously. 'Well, I suppose I must awa'.'

'Oh aye?' I said. 'But thou need na start awa sae hasty wi' bickering brattle! I wad be laith to rin an' chase thee . . .' But she had already disappeared.

A Merry Christmas

Until the beginning of December I had been getting along quite nicely, then all of a sudden preparations for Christmas started to appear. Paper-chains and other forms of decoration began to go up and sprigs of mistletoe were dotted about in the ward, giving rise to outbursts of embarrassing facetiousness. Balloons and tinsel also made their appearance. Being in the lavatory at the time, I was unable to prevent two pale pink balloons from being hung up above my bed. Dr Robertshaw, when he saw them, looked at them meditatively.

'I don't think much of those for decorations,' he said. 'Still, I suppose they might do as a substitute for female company.'

The *chef d'oeuvre* of the decorations was, or was intended to be, a large holly wreath which was suspended from the ceiling. It was less effective than it might have been if Matron, making a tour of the ward, had not inadvertently sat down on it before it was put up. I was told that she had been rushed to Casualty and that a bulletin issued later said that she was doing as well as could be expected.

Presently I began to hear ominous talk among the nurses about a 'patients' party'. Would I be expected to go to it, I wondered. The prospect didn't bear thinking about. If there is one thing that fills me with misgiving, it is having to indulge, willy-nilly, in corporate jollity with strangers; for although by this time I had established a nodding acquaintance with several of the patients in the ward, I would not have put our relationship on a more intimate footing than that.

'What exactly happens?' I asked Susie, dreading the answer.

She explained that all those patients who were in a fit state to do so, would be sent back to their homes for the two or three days of Christmas, and the rest, those too far gone to be packed off, would, unless actually *in extremis*, be making merry among themselves, with various members of the staff helping to jolly things along and make them go with a swing. From the way she described the affair, I don't know which seemed the more heroic, the efforts of the nurses or of the patients.

'And will you be attending this orgy?' I said.

'You bet. Why, aren't you coming?'

'I think not,' I said.

'They'll be ever so disappointed if you don't.'

'I don't think I could stand the excitement,' I said. 'I like it here in Thoracic: I don't want to have to be transferred to Cardiac.'

Susie looked at me scornfully. 'Pooh,' she said. 'Besides, there's the Christmas lunch – you must come to the lunch. They'll be having turkey and Christmas pudding and mince pies and all that. And there's always masses to drink.'

Even the prospect of unlimited liquor failed to move me.

'Frankly,' I said, 'I'm not very good at Christmas. I think you'd much better count me out.'

'Get away, you'd enjoy it, you know you would.'

'I'm not altogether convinced of that,' I said.

'Well, we'll see.'

A few days before Christmas, at about six o'clock in the evening, I was playing a game of patience and revelling in my solitude, when I heard a sort of shuffling going on in the corridor outside, a sound, as it were, of elfin footsteps, and the next thing I knew was that my privacy had been invaded by a posse of carol singers. They were dressed, if you please, in Victorian costume, and one or two, despite the fact that all the lights were on, were carrying lanterns. Without a word to me, this ghastly crew formed up round my bed, and their leader, a man quite old enough to have known better, and wearing a broad-brimmed top-hat several sizes too large for him, struck a tuning fork on the heel of his boot and off they went into 'The First Noel'.

I was absolutely dumbfounded. The whole thing was so unexpected. And I was not less amazed when they changed their tune to 'God Rest Ye Merry Gentlemen' and the leader, looking me full in the face, and obviously oblivious to the irony of the situation, bawled out 'Let nothing you dismay!'

After two or three more sacred ditties, they brought their carolling to a close with what we used to call at school 'While Shepherds Washed Their Socks by Night', and then the party trooped out. At the door their smug-faced leader turned and raised his huge hat.

'Good night,' he said.

'Good *night*!' I said.

For the next quarter of an hour or so I heard them warbling away to the other patients, and then they all shuffled out, presumably to inflict their melodies on the unfortunate captives of some other ward.

Christmas Day dawned and with it, bright and early, came Mr Dring on his routine tour of inspection.

'You're joining us for lunch, I hear,' he said.

Making a mental note to wring Susie's neck at the earliest opportunity, I sought to parry his implied suggestion.

'Well, it depends on what time my wife arrives,' I said. (We had arranged between us, Madeleine and I, that she would so contrive matters as to arrive just in time to prevent my joining the revels.)

Mr Dring looked disapproving. 'I think you ought to try and put in an appearance,' he said. 'Besides, it'll do you good.'

What could have given him that idea, I could not imagine.

'Will you be there?' I asked.

'I shall look in, just to carve the turkey, then I have to return to the bosom of my family.'

Crafty, I thought.

Promptly at twelve-thirty Madeleine arrived, and never had I been more delighted to see her. She came, bless her, laden with presents, most of them not of the slightest use to me in hospital.

'Still, it's the spirit that counts,' I said, and I opened the bottle of Glenlivet that she had brought for me.

I was woken from an alcoholic sleep at about four o'clock by sounds of revelry without. A sing-song seemed to be in progress in the ward, crackers were being pulled, and now and then there were bursts of hilarious laughter.

Soon after I had woken up, Susie brought me in my tea.

'What on earth's going on out there?' I asked.

'Party,' she said. 'Coming to join us?'

I had had no such intention, but now a complication arose in the form of a call of nature. And so, I put on my dressing gown, and with Susie toting my jar, made with what speed I could for the lavatory.

If I had expected to be greeted with black looks, with disapproving comments on my failure to join in the general merry-making, I need have had no such apprehensions. The ward was crammed

Relations with the Church

with noisy relatives and both they and the patients, even those that were in bed, seemed to be having a whale of a time. All were wearing paper hats and not a few had got on funny noses. Several seemed as tight as ticks, though not the Reverend Dobbs, who was standing chatting to a group of relatives. True, he was weaving about a bit, but he did that anyway, and had a fixed and fatuous smile on his face, but sobriety was written there too in large letters. In the midst of all this gaiety my presence happily went completely unnoticed.

As I came out of the lavatory I ran into Jam, standing alone and looking rather out of things. He was wearing a Punchinello cap back to front. Seeing me, he pressed his palms together and bowed.

'May I be permitted to offer you greetings, sah, on this festive occasion,' he said gravely.

I bowed too. 'Salaam, I—'

'Salami?' said Yvonne, who was passing at that moment with a plate of mince pies. 'Good gracious, you've had turkey and trimmings and Lord knows what, now he's asking for salami. You are an old greedy guts, aren't you?'

She beamed merrily upon us. I noticed that she seemed slightly flushed and that there was a hint of a slur in her speech, so I said nothing and she went on her way.

On the other side of the ward a rowdy group had started off on 'Knees Up, Mother Brown'. As I watched them reeling backwards and forwards, I could see what was coming. On the backward swing one of them cannoned into the Reverend Dobbs, who, caught entirely unawares, went face down onto a patient's bed, sending the patient, who was perched on the edge on the other side, into the lap of an elderly relative sitting by the bed, who pitched over sideways and to break his fall, clutched the covers of the bed bext door, sending a tea-tray crashing to the floor.

I did not wait to see the culmination of this chain-reaction, but took up my jar and walked. As I reached the door of my room, I saw Deirdre of the Sorrows being supported from the ward by two of the patients.

'What's the matter with her?' I asked O'Grady, who was bringing up the rear.

'Ah, she's a drop taken. She'll be all right. Here, oi've not wisht yer a Happy Christmas yet,' and side-stepping my jar, O'Grady saluted me with a whacking whisky-laden kiss.

At supper time that evening I asked Susie how things had gone at lunch.

'Oh, it was a barrel of fun,' she said. 'But Mr Dring, the way he hacked that turkey about! He needs a lesson in carving.'

Dr Dolan had said he would remove my stitches on Boxing Day. There were forty-four to take out, so I imagined the process might be a fairly long one.

'I hope you're not coming in specially on Boxing Day to take them out.'

'No, I'll be at the Children's Party anyway,' he said. 'So I'll come along after that.'

And so he did; and skilfully, painlessly, he removed my stitches, dressed as Father Christmas.

The Order of Release

About a fortnight after Christmas, Mr Dring pronounced me fit to return to civilization. I could hardly believe it. I felt utterly bewildered, sharing for a few minutes the sensations of Doctor Manette on his release from the Bastille.

'But what will it be like out there?' I asked, trying to hide my agitation. 'Everything must have changed tremendously. Shall I be able to understand what people say? And will they be able to understand me?'

Dr Dring was reassuring. I should find life, he said, much the same as before. The politicians were still blackguarding each other, making cheap party capital out of the other's misfortunes; the Burtons had parted yet again, then had come together, but were now once more apart; *The Mousetrap* was still running; the pound in your pocket was still worth 48p; and there was still an unofficial strike on British Rail. It was all very comforting. For a moment I had had visions of returning to a world from which all the familiar faces and institutions had faded away.

'We'll arrange for you to go next Thursday, then,' said Mr Dring. 'Better make it the afternoon.'

I awaited Madeleine's arrival that day almost faint with excitement.

'Guess what!' I shouted the moment she appeared.

'They're going to give you another endoscopy?'

'I'm coming home.'

'When?'

'On Thursday.'

'In the morning or the afternoon?'

'In the afternoon.'

'You can't do that,' she said. 'I'm having my hair done.'

Eventually I persuaded her to change her appointment and just as I released the arm-lock Sister Forbes appeared with some tea.

'So you're leaving us, I hear,' she said. 'There's gratitude for you.'

'It breaks my heart, Sister,' I said, 'but I just can't go on being such a burden to you.' There's many a true word spoken in jest and this I felt to be one of them. 'Could you arrange, incidentally, for an ambulance to take me home?'

'An ambulance? What d'you want an ambulance for? You're supposed to be a fit man now.'

'You must be out of your medical mind,' I cried. 'Look at me, if you can bear to, pathetically weazened object that I am. I haven't got the strength of a rabbit.'

'There are other resemblances,' said Madeleine.

'You keep out of this,' I said. 'Sister, I must have an ambulance – *please*.'

Sister Forbes turned to my wife. 'Why can't you drive him home?' she said.

'Because I don't want to end up in hospital again,' I said. 'Sister, please—'

When Thursday afternoon came, with it came two stalwart ambulance men, one to carry my bag (I suppose I could have carried my tooth-brush, but it didn't seem worth while not to pack it) and the various other things I had accumulated during my stay; my radio, a basket of books, a pineapple, and some assorted bottles of booze. And so at last, after nearly eight weeks, I was homeward bound. Freedom lay on the horizon.

I gave a last look round my little room to make sure that I was leaving nothing behind; nothing of any consequence, that is. There were a few back numbers of *The Economist*, but these I decided to leave; they might bring a touch of fun, I thought, to the lonely vigil of the night sister.

To this moment of release I had been looking forward with the avid expectancy of a shipwrecked mariner sighting rescue. Yet now that my deliverance was at hand there descended on me a sudden reluctance to depart. Once more I was assailed by doubts and apprehensions. How should I fare in the harsh, competitive world to which I was about to return? Where would I find the strong supporting arm, the reassuring smile, the kindly word that had meant so much to me in my weakened state? Madeleine's arm wasn't all that strong, nor her smile invariably reassuring, and somehow her kindly words had a tendency to sound ironic. Faced with a prospect of helpless isolation in a strange and hostile environment, panic seized me; and then, Sister Forbes, entering briskly, did the same.

'Come on, time you were off.'

She bundled me outside into the ward and with ambulance men in close attendance, I led a stately procession to the door, still feeling exceedingly unsteady on my pins and looking like a wild and emaciated tramp. As we passed on our way, a feeble cheer went up from the patients, some lying in their beds, a few lounging in their pyjamas. For some this respiratory effort was more than they could stand and their hurrahs faded away in spasms of coughing and spitting.

We came out into the darkness – it was now half-past five – where the ambulance was waiting a few yards away.

'Mind the step,' the ambulance man said, as I emerged.

Both of them put down what they were carrying to help me to my feet, then guided me to the ambulance.

I am not, I hope, a sentimentalist, but thoughts of hearth and home, from which I had been separated for so long, brought quite a lump to my throat. It was a good thing I still had my plastic sputum cup with me.

The lights were on in the house as we approached. It was a welcome sight, but I was in for a shock. Madeleine had not told me that she had asked her sister Millicent to stay; it was Millicent who opened the front door.

'So you're back at last,' she said. 'I had no idea an endoscopy took so long.'